THE NEW RANGER

BY MARILYN EASTON

SCHOLASTIC INC.

New York   Toronto   London   Auckland
Sydney   Mexico City   New Delhi   Hong Kong

ISBN 978-0-545-39008-8

12 11 10 9 8 7 6 5 4 3 2 1   12 13 14 15 16/0
Printed in the U.S.A.   40
First printing, January 2012

One afternoon, the **Power Rangers** were at the Shiba House. Suddenly, they heard a strange noise coming from outside. Jayden went to see what was going on and found an arrow stuck in the wall.

"It says, 'See you soon,'" said **Jayden**.

"There's something fishy about this," Mike said. "No, seriously. This note smells fishy," he explained.

"You four go to the docks and see what you can find," Jayden directed. "I'll stay here in case something happens."

While at the docks, a young man selling fish handed **Emily** a flyer. The writing on the flyer looked familiar.

"Can I see the note that was attached to the arrow?" Emily asked **Mia**. The writing on both pieces of paper was exactly the same!

"Well, that's fishy," Mike said.

The **Rangers** approached the young man selling fish. "Did you make these flyers?" Mia asked the man. "Yep, that's me. I'm **Antonio**," he replied.

"Well, it sure is nicer to have one handed to you than shot at you," Emily said.

"That's for sure!" Antonio added. But then he realized he was talking to the **Power Rangers**!

"Uh-oh!" he yelled as he sped away, tipping over a bucket of ice to trip up the Rangers.

Mike's Samuraizer rang just as Antonio dashed off.
"There's a **Nighlok** in Spring Valley!" Mentor Ji said.
"Go help Jayden!"
With that, the Power Rangers ran to help their friend.

In Spring Valley, the Rangers found themselves face-to-face with **Vulpes**, a master of mirror spells. "Let's send this Nighlok back where he belongs," said the Red Ranger.

The Rangers spun their **Power Discs** on their swords.

"Spin Sword Quintuple Slash!" the **Red Ranger** called. Vulpes acted fast, and cast a spell that sent the Rangers' slash attack right back at them.

Vulpes' spell was so powerful that it knocked the **Rangers** to the ground and made them demorph. Now that they were back to normal, they were too weak to fight.

"I have **thousands** of mirror spells," said Vulpes. "I can handle whatever you throw my way. But I know you can't handle what I'm about to throw at you!"

A barrage of **barracuda bombs** interrupted Vulpes. "What about what I throw at you?" a voice called from the woods. The Rangers turned and saw it was **Antonio**, the guy from the docks.

"What's he doing here?" asked Jayden.

The Rangers got their answer when Antonio morphed into the **Gold Ranger**!

"Don't worry, guys, just leave this Nighlok to me!" he said. "**Gold Power**!"

How could this be? They never knew about a sixth Samurai Ranger!

Before the Rangers could react, Vulpes sent a group of **Moogers** to attack the Gold Ranger. In a flash, the Gold Ranger defeated them all.

"How did he do that? He didn't even move!" said Mia.

"Yes, he did," replied Jayden. "Just faster than the eye can see. Looks like he is the first Ranger to master the legendary **Sheath Slash Maneuver**."

Now the **Gold Ranger** set his sights on Vulpes. The Gold Ranger unsheathed his **Barracuda Blade**. Then he charged at the Nighlok.

With just a few slashes of the Gold Ranger's blade, the **Nighlok** was defeated.

But each Nighlok has a second life as a **MegaMonster**! "You haven't seen anything yet!" Vulpes said as he grew into a gigantic version of himself.

The Rangers pulled out their **Samuraizers** and morphed into Mega Mode.

First the Rangers combined their zords into the Samurai Megazord. Then they combined with the Samurai Battlewing to form the **Battlewing Megazord**!

Now the Rangers were ready to fight, but Vulpes had a surprise for them.

"Vulpes Veil," the Nighlok shouted as he disappeared.

The **Gold Ranger** wanted to help so he grabbed his Samuraizer and texted the **OctoZord** to come to the rescue.

Then the Gold Ranger morphed into Mega Mode and entered the OctoZord cockpit.

"Alright, **Vulpes**!" shouted the Gold Ranger. "Come out, come out, wherever you are! **Octo Ink Cloud**!"
Then the OctoZord shot out a cloud of ink. Now the Nighlok was visible again!

The Rangers took this chance to strike their final blow.
"Oh, no!" Vulpes cried as he was defeated.
"**Victory** is ours!" cheered the Rangers.

"Alright, **Gold Ranger**," said Kevin. "What's your story? Who are you?"

"Guys, this is my friend Antonio!" **Jayden** explained. "We were friends when we were children. I gave him the OctoZord when he moved away. That way he'd always remember our friendship."

The old friends were reunited and celebrated with some practice sparring for fun. The Power Rangers now had another member of their team! **Go, Gold!**